RIDER WOOFSON

THE SOCCER BALL MONSTER MYSTERY

BY WALKER STYLES ● ILLUSTRATED BY BEN WHITEHOUSE

LITTLE SIMON

New York London Toronto Sydney New Delhi

LITTLE SIMON

An imprint of Simon & Schuster Children's Publishing Division
1230 Avenue of the Americas, New York, New York 10020
First Little Simon hardcover edition October 2016
Copyright © 2016 by Simon & Schuster, Inc.
For information about special discounts for bulk purchases, please contact Simon & Schuster Special Sales at 1-866-506-1949 or business@simonandschuster.com. The Simon & Schuster Speakers Bureau can bring authors to your live event. For more information or to book an event contact the Simon & Schuster Speakers Bureau at 1-866-248-3049 or visit our website at www.simonspeakers.com.
Designed by Laura Roode. The text of this book was set in ITC American Typewriter.
Manufactured in the United States of America 0916 FFG
2 4 6 8 10 9 7 5 3 1
Library of Congress Cataloging-in-Publication Data
Names: Styles, Walker, author. | Whitehouse, Ben, illustrator. | Title: The soccer ball monster mystery / by Walker Styles ; illustrated by Ben Whitehouse. | Description: First Little Simon paperback edition. | New York : Little Simon, 2016. | Series: Rider Woofson ; 6 | Summary: Rider and the P.I. Pack try to find the soccer team's missing mascot, Dynamo Dog. | Identifiers: LCCN 2016010287 | ISBN 9781481471107 (pbk) | ISBN 9781481471114 (hc) | ISBN 9781481471121 (eBook) | Subjects: | CYAC: Mystery and detective stories. | Detectives—Fiction. | Dogs—Fiction. | Mascots—Fiction. | Soccer—Fiction. | BISAC: JUVENILE FICTION / Readers / Chapter Books. | JUVENILE FICTION / Action & Adventure / General. | JUVENILE FICTION / Animals / General. Classification: LCC PZ7.1.S82 Sm 2016 | DDC [Fic]—dc23 LC record available at https://lccn.loc.gov/2016010287

CONTENTS

chapter
ONE

7 ★PD
DAVID GECKOM

CC
10
10 ★CC
LION L.MESSY

SOCCER FANS

"Are you kidding?" barked Ziggy Fluffenscruff. "David Geckom is *the* number one player in the All-Star Soccer League. He'll totally get voted MVP this year!"

"Kid, I wish you were right, but you don't know what you're talking about," Rora Gooddog said with a laugh. "Lion L. Messy has won it the last two years in a row. Maybe third time's the charm."

Ziggy and Rora were dog detectives and members of the Pup Investigators Pack. They didn't always see eye to eye, but they did have two things in common:

They both loved to solve crimes, and they were both crazy about soccer—especially their hometown team, the Pawston Dynamos!

"I've never seen you two this excited about the same thing," Rider Woofson noted. Rider was

their boss, and the leader of the P.I. Pack. "What sport are you talking about?"

"*Bow-wowza*, Boss! This is only the most important sport in the history of the planet!" Ziggy's tail wagged excitedly. "Soccer!"

"This weekend is the big championship match between the Pawston Dynamos and the Catskills Cougars," Rora added. "We both have front row seats."

Together, the two dogs cheered:

*"We rock! We rule!
We like to school these
fools!*

*We're no average Joe's—
we're the Pawston
Dynamos!"*

Rider had a good chuckle as his two teammates began kicking a soccer ball back and forth in the office space. But Ziggy, the youngest pup in the group, was riled up and kicked the ball too hard. It hit a coat rack, bounced off the ceiling fan, and crashed into a huge pillow fort on the other side of the room.

The pillow-and-blanket fort was covered in signs that read TOP SECRET! and KEEP OUT! and GENIUS AT WORK! But now half of the front wall was crumbled.

"Uh-oh, kid," Rora said to her fellow soccer fan. "We'd better make a run for it."

Westie Barker—a brilliant inventor, and the fourth member of the team—popped out and growled. "I ask very little of you, my friends, except that you stay clear of my brainstorm fortress when I'm in

the middle of building a creation!"

"Sorry, Westie," Ziggy said. "We were talking about soccer, and I just got *soooo* excited!"

"Yes, well, I'm excited too. . . . I'm working on a new invention!" Westie barked.

"What is it?" Rider asked. He glimpsed a machine with dozens of mechanical legs like a caterpillar.

Westie quickly fixed the fallen blanket to cover the mysterious gadget. "I'm not ready to say. Not just yet. These things take time. Now, please, if you don't mind"— the terrier tossed the soccer ball back to his friend—"keep my inventing space clear of any and all hockey balls!"

"Hockey ball?!" Ziggy snorted. "There's no such thing!"

"We'll let Westie have that one,"

Rider said with a smile. "Let's go have a soccer match in the park and give our inventor some peace and quiet."

"Great idea, Boss," Rora said. "Hey, I have an extra ticket to the game if you'd like to join us."

"Thanks. That sounds swell." Rider nodded. "After all, it's not often that the P.I. Pack sees a fair match."

chapter TWO

GO, GO, DYNAMOS!

At the Pet Life Stadium, the Pawston Dynamos were out on the field, practicing for the big game. The players ran through some warm-up drills while their coaches barked orders and advice.

Seated in the stadium box, three more soccer fans were watching. The Pawston mayor cheered on the

Dynamos while Pawston's richest cat, Mr. Meow, glared at the home team. By their side was Frenchie, a dog who was chosen by the police to be the head of soccer-stadium security.

"I know that look, Mr. Meow," the mayor said. "I thought you liked soccer?"

"I love *ssssoccer*," Mr. Meow hissed, "but I'm pulling for the best team, the Catskillssss Cougarsssss, not these dim-witted Dynamossss." He pulled out a Cougars scarf and wrapped it proudly around his neck.

The mayor let out a tremendous laugh. "As long as it's a good game this weekend, I don't care who wins!" Then, with a wink, he added, "Though, Pawston should handle those Cougars easily enough, especially if Dynamo Dog is here to cheer on the team!"

At that moment, a muscular dog with a square jaw stepped onto the field dressed in tights, a cape, and a mask.

"Don't you fear!
Dynamo Dog is here!

Here to cheer! Goooooo,
Pawston Dynamos!"

Then there was an explosion of fireworks behind him.

The whole team cheered and clapped. Frenchie and the mayor each whistled with excitement too. Even Mr. Meow was mesmerized by Dynamo Dog's *bow-wow-wow* factor!

"Go, Pawsssston!" the cat shouted— before catching himself. "Oh, I mean . . . Go, Cougars!"

"Don't worry," Frenchie said. "It happens all the time. That's the sort of thing Dynamo Dog does to

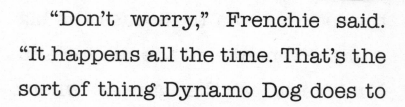

fans of any team. If you follow me, I'll show you all the security we will have in place for this weekend to make sure everyone has a safe and fun time."

When practice ended, the soccer team followed the coaches into the locker room to discuss the big game. Frenchie led the mayor and Mr. Meow to the garage where

their cars were waiting. The only person left on the field was the team mascot, Dynamo Dog.

He was almost done, but he still had his special signature move left to practice. Dynamo Dog pushed a button on his cape, and his entire outfit began to glow.

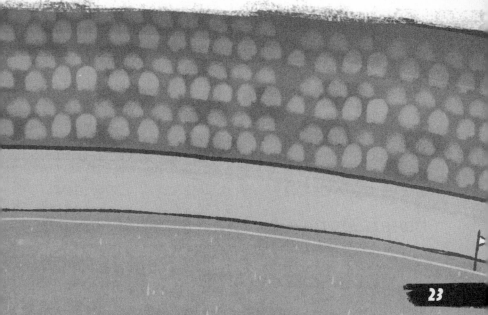

He raced toward the goal, did a somersault, a triple back flip, and . . . landed in a bag held by a giant Soccer Ball Monster with mean eyes and a dark grin!

That was definitely not the way his special signature move was supposed to end!

Dynamo Dog tried to get out of the bag, but the menacing monster tied the open end shut. Then it cackled an evil laugh as it dragged the mascot away. Dynamo Dog had been Dynamo *Dog-napped*!

chapter
THREE

THE MISSING MASCOT

The P.I. Pack raced to the soccer stadium as soon as the mayor called with the bad news about Pawston's missing mascot.

"Oh, poor Dynamo Dog," Ziggy whined, hiding his face in his paws.

"I think poor Pawston Dynamos is more like it," corrected Rora.

"The team needs their mascot now more than ever! How could this happen before the big game?"

"I know. It's awful!" Frenchie moaned. The security dog was biting his nails. "Being in charge of the big game was supposed to be my big break with the police

force. Now it's looking like my big break-*away* from the police force. They're gonna fire me for sure!"

"Not if we can help it," Rider said. "First thing's first, what can you tell me about last night? Who was the last person to see Dynamo Dog?"

"That would have been me," said David Geckom. The skinny gecko was the star

player of the Pawston Dynamos soccer team. Rora and Ziggy were instantly awe-struck meeting him in real life. For once, both detectives were at a loss for words. "Coach and I were running through a training routine. We were the last ones off the soccer pitch besides Dynamo."

"The soccer what?" asked Rider.

"The pitch is what soccer players call the field," Ziggy blurted out.

"That's right," Geckom said with a smile, and Ziggy nearly fainted. "So when we left, Dynamo Dog was practicing some of his famous routines. He was supposed to join us for dinner afterward, but he never showed up. We came back this morning, and he was nowhere to be found."

"Are you sure he's not just late to practice?" Rider asked.

"I'm sure," said the head coach as he joined the crew. "Dynamo Dog has never been late in his life. He knows that this team depends on him."

"Okay, the next step is—" Rider began, but he was suddenly interrupted.

"Autographs!" Ziggy shouted, unable to contain his super-fan excitement any longer. Ziggy shoved his Pawston Dynamos cap at David Geckom. "Can you please sign this? Say, 'To my number one fan!'"

Then Rora pushed Ziggy aside. "Pardon my friend. He's so silly. *I'm* your number one fan."

"What? That's not true!" Ziggy shouted.

The two detectives swatted each other while trying to win Geckom's attention. The soccer player just laughed. "You're both very sweet. I'm sorry to run, but I need to practice if we're going to beat those Cougars."

"Good job, kid. You scared him off," Rora huffed.

"No, I didn't! You did!" Ziggy argued.

"Enough, you two," Rider said. "We have a missing mascot and a crime to solve. Let's start sniffing out some clues."

"I'm already on it!" Westie

said. He was holding a large metal cone over his nose and was sniffing around the field. "I'm using one of my new inventions: the Super Sniffer 2000. It triples my sense of smell. And right now, I smell . . . a lion?"

Westie put his nose down and followed the strange scent. He sniffed across the field, sniffed over by the goal, then sniffed up and down the

stands. Finally, he turned a corner, and discovered their first clue—a team uniform from the Catskills Cougars! It was hidden next to the practice area!

"Good job, Westie," said Rora. "It looks like your nose wasn't lying about smelling that lion. Anyone feel like taking a trip to the Catskills? I think this mystery just became *messy*."

YOU'RE NOT LION

The P.I. Pack drove to the Catskills, a town in the mountains just outside of Pawston. They arrived at the Cougars' stadium as the team was breaking for lunch. The clue Westie had found tipped Rora off that the Catskills Cougars may be part of this mystery. She wanted to talk to the player who wore

number ten. His name was Lion
L. Messy, and he was the Cougars'
star player.

"Mind if we ask you a few ques-
tions?" Rider asked.

"Of course not," Messy said. The
lion soccer star was very polite.

"I heard about Dynamo Dog, and I am happy to help in any way I can."

"A-ha! You said you were happy!" Rora pointed at Messy. "Admit it! *You* took Dynamo Dog so that the Cougars could win the championship and you'd be named the MVP for the third year in a row!"

"Careful, Detective," Rider said to Rora, motioning for her to step back from Messy. "I think your soccer *craze* is turning *crazy*. Let's hear what Mr. Messy has to say."

"I am sorry about what happened, but it was not me," Messy claimed. "I was being interviewed on TV last night by the news."

Westie pulled out his phone and began pawing at the screen. "He's telling the truth. Mr. Messy is innocent."

"We're sorry to have troubled you," Rider apologized.

"It is no trouble," Messy said.

"Then perhaps it would also be no trouble to sign

a few items for me?" Ziggy said,
pushing Rider and Rora out of
the way. "I have a poster, some
stickers, your playing card, a hat,
a soccer ball, a T-shirt, a sweat-
shirt, a scarf, some shin guards,
a pair of dirty socks, your team
jersey, some cleats, a pair of soccer shorts, one goalie glove—"

"*Bow-wowza!*" Rora shouted Ziggy's catchphrase. "Where did all that stuff come from, kid?"

While Messy was signing everything for Ziggy, Westie wandered over to the other end of the field with his Super Sniffer 2000. "Hey, team! I sniffed out another clue."

"Looks like at least one detective here is going for MVP," Rider said, patting Ziggy and Rora on the back. "What did you find?"

Westie held up a Dynamos uniform. Rider turned to Messy. "Hmmm, is anyone on your team missing?"

"No," said Messy. "Everyone is here, including our mascot."

"Have you seen anything odd

or strange?" asked Rora. "I mean, besides Ziggy."

"Nothing," Messy confirmed.

Rider and the team thanked the soccer star as they left—except Rora, who whispered, "I'm keeping an eye on you!"

Once Messy was alone, he juggled the last ball on the pitch and raced toward the goal. He spun around pretend defenders and then kicked the ball to score. Suddenly, the net from the soccer goal reached out and grabbed Messy. He was trapped. "I've netted a goal before, but I've never netted myself!" he cried. "Someone, please help!"

Then the Soccer Ball Monster came out and roared an evil laugh. The monster grabbed the netting with Messy inside and carried the superstar off the pitch.

chapter
FIVE

KICKING AND STOMPING

Back at the P.I. Pack office, the detectives learned the news about Lion L. Messy's disappearance.

"Now I feel bad for thinking Messy was guilty," Rora said.

"Don't feel bad for him. Feel bad for us," Ziggy moaned. "The big game is in just a few days. It won't be the same without the greatest mascot and the soccer MVP playing."

"Let's get our heads back in the game—the *detective* game," Rider said, taking charge. "Two animals are missing, and we need to find them."

Ziggy looked at everything signed by Lion L. Messy on his desk. "You're right, Boss. I was being selfish. We need to solve this case."

Still, Ziggy and Rora seemed to come down with a case of the blahs.

"I know what will cheer you up," Westie said. "I'll show you my top secret invention. I call it—the Kooky Kicker."

Westie pulled a sheet away to reveal a machine with a kick line of robotic legs. He pressed a button on his remote control, and the legs began to kick. "My Kooky Kicker cleans up messes by kicking them away. Watch."

The strange machine shuffled around the office. First, it kicked books from the floor back onto the shelf in alphabetical order. Then, it kicked some stray pieces of trash back into the trash can. It even kicked files back into their correct cabinets.

"Well, isn't that just hunky-dory," Rora said with a smile. "I need one of those at my place."

Suddenly, the lights on the machine turned from green to red. Instead of kicking, it began stomping. The Kooky Kicker began flattening everything in sight and then kicking it under the rug.

"Oh my!" Westie said

as he dropped his remote. "It looks like my Kooky Kicker has some kooky kinks to work out." Together, the team jumped on the invention, riding it like a bucking bronco until Westie managed to flip the off switch on the robot.

"Whew, that was a close one!"

"My Messy memorabilia got all messed up!" Ziggy moaned. "Could this week get any worse?!"

Suddenly, the office door burst open. Frenchie walked proudly into the room and boldly announced,

"I know what happened to both Dynamo Dog and Lion L. Messy! It's the Goalie's Curse!"

THE GOALIE'S CURSE

"A curse!" Ziggy said with his eyes widening. "Don't curses come with ghosts and monsters?!"

"There's no such thing as curses, *or* ghosts, *or* monsters," Rider said seriously.

"I don't know, Boss," Rora said. "I have a good luck charm, and when I don't bring it to a game, my favorite team always loses. If you believe in luck, then bad luck can be the same as a curse."

"Hear me out," Frenchie said to Rider. "Legend says there was once a young goalie who devoted his entire life to soccer. When he finished school, he tried out for

the big leagues. He didn't make it onto either the Dynamos or the Cougars, so he swore revenge on both teams. That's where the Goalie's Curse comes from! This goalie promised that if both teams ever made it to the championship, *neither* team would win. The

teams have never made it into the championship at the same time . . . until this year."

"*Bow-wowza!*" Ziggy said. "It *is* the curse!"

Rider rolled his eyes. "Sounds like a soccer legend to me, not a curse. What we need to do is stick to the facts and clues that we know."

"The only clues we have are a

Cougars uniform at the Dynamos field, and a Dynamos uniform at the Cougars field," Rora pointed out. "Sounds to me like both teams are in trouble. Maybe it really is the Goalie's Curse."

"It's not a curse," Rider stated.

"I don't know," Westie said. "There are things even science cannot explain."

"Not you too," Rider said to his friend. "Whoever did this is a real-life criminal who is going to spend time behind real-life bars."

"I hope you're right," Frenchie

said. "I can't stand the idea of a real-life curse!"

"Well, correct me if I'm wrong," Rider pointed out. "The curse is meant to stop either team from winning, right? Well, even though one player and one mascot are missing, the teams can still play. Nothing is going to stop the champion- ship game. If the curse were real, then some- thing would have to completely stop the game from ever happening."

Frenchie's phone rang. He answered it and heard someone shouting on the other end. When the pup hung up, Frenchie looked pale, as though he had talked to a ghost. "That was the mayor," Frenchie said. "There's been another incident at the stadium. All the seat number

stickers were removed and scattered across the field."

"The curse!" Rora, Ziggy, and
Westie shouted at the same time.

A STICKY SITUATION

When the P.I. Pack arrived at the Pet Life Stadium, the mayor and Mr. Meow were covered in seat number stickers. Both of them were running back and forth between the field and the stadium seats.

"Don't jus*ssss*t *ssss*tand there! Help u*ssss*!" cried Mr. Meow as he tried to separate the stickers covering his paws. The mayor was running in circles, chasing a sticker on the end of his tail.

"What happened?" Rider asked as he helped the mayor.

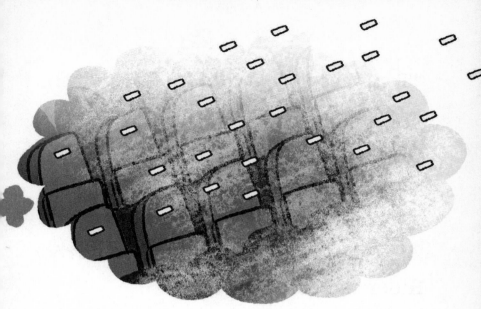

"We have no clue!" the mayor said. "One minute everything was normal, and then there was a terrible fog and a gust of wind, and all the seat number stickers flew onto the field."

"Is that bad?" Rider said.

"It's terrible!" the mayor cried.

"Tomorrow's game is sold out! Fans for both teams have their tickets, but they'll never find their seats if we don't get every single sticker back onto its correct place!"

"Who could have done this?" Rider asked.

"Who caressss?!" Mr. Meow hissed. "Without sssseats, there won't be a game."

"I think I can help!" Westie said. He pulled out the remote to his Kooky Kicker. Rora and Westie flinched. "Don't worry. I made some adjustments on the ride over here. It should be fine."

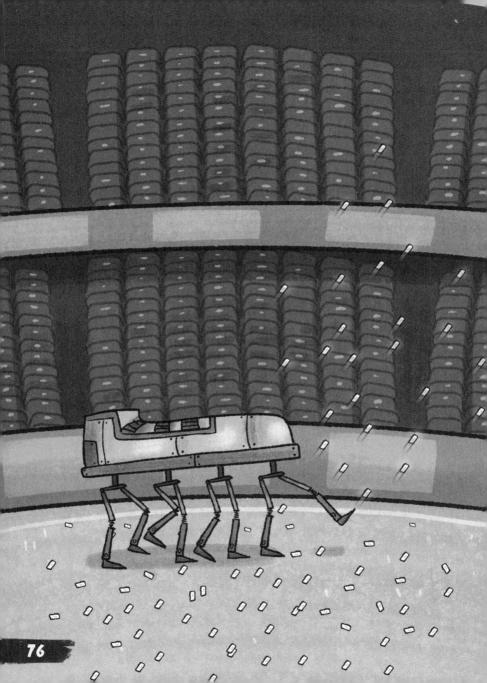

Westie pushed the on switch, and within seconds the mechanical legs ran into the stadium! *Kick! Kick! Kick! Kick! Kick! Kick! Kick!* It was kicking stickers left and right. In only a few minutes, the Kooky Kicker had kicked and fixed all of the ninety thousand seat stickers.

The mayor and Mr. Meow ran across the field and hugged Westie.

"You *ssss*aved the champion-*sssss*hip game!" Mr. Meow said.

"You saved the day!" the mayor shouted.

"Thanks, Westie." Rider held up the dirty soccer shirt. "But there's still a case to solve."

An alarm went off inside Rora's head. "Oh no!" she said, pointing to the shirt. "Where's David Geckom?"

"You mean lucky number seven? He's over there," the mayor said.

"Hurry, gang," Rora said as she ran quickly toward the Dynamos players on the other side of the soccer field. "I think I know who's about to get gecko-napped next!"

"How?" Ziggy, Westie, and Rider asked, chasing after her.

"The numbers on the uniforms we found! The first one led us to Lion L. Messy, who was lion-napped. Well, the jersey we found in the Catskills was Geckom's number under all that dirt."

"Oh no! Not Geckom, too!" Ziggy shouted in a panic. "Foul ball! It's too late!"

The P.I. Pack stopped in their tracks. There was a Soccer Ball Monster on the field.

The Dynamos players saw it and scattered. Only David Geckom stood his ground. "I'm not afraid of a giant soccer ball!" he shouted. "It's my job to kick balls like you all across the country!"

The giant monster charged toward Geckom. He was ready

to knock the ball out of the park
when the Kooky Kicker tripped
the soccer star by mistake!

CHOMP!

The monster's mouth swallowed
the gecko in one gulp.

chapter
EIGHT

SOCCER BALL MONSTER MATCH

"That Soccer Ball Monster just ate David Geckom!" Westie barked. "And it's all my invention's fault!"

"There is no such thing as a monster," Rider said.

"Try telling that to him!" shouted Westie as the giant soccer ball began chasing the other Dynamos players. Its mouth opened and closed like a mechanical crocodile. *Chomp! Chomp! Chomp!*

"Monster or not," Ziggy said as he pushed up his sleeves. "I've had enough of this nonsense. Let's take that Soccer Ball Monster down!"

"I'm with you, kid!" Rora said. "No one messes with my favorite game and gets away with it!"

The P.I. Pack surrounded the Soccer Ball Monster. Westie pulled out a net and launched it at the monster—but he missed. Rider tried to tackle the monster, but it threw him off with ease. Even Frenchie tried to help, but all he did was trip over his own feet and get trapped in Westie's net.

Then Ziggy and Rora made a grab for the beast, but the Soccer Ball Monster rolled away.

Mr. Meow and the mayor ran to join the fight too. "Rider Woofson, you have to fix this!" the mayor panted.

"I'm trying, Mr. Mayor," Rider admitted. "But how in the world do you defeat a giant soccer ball?!"

"That's the ticket!" Rora winked at Ziggy.

The young pup detective smiled and pointed to his foot. "The way to defeat a Soccer Ball Monster is by using *de-feet*!"

"Then let's show off *our* soccer skills!" Rora coached.

The pair of detectives raced after the giant soccer ball. Rora got in front of it and gave it a hard kick. The monster flew up way into the air. Then Rora passed the ball back to Ziggy, who bounced it on his knee.

The detectives kicked the monster back and forth, dribbling it down the field. As they approached the goal, Rora shouted to her teammate, "Are you ready?!"

"I'll set you up for the trick shot!" Ziggy yelled back.

Rora nodded, then Ziggy passed the giant soccer ball to her. She flipped over backward and smacked the monster right into the back of the net. It was a perfect bicycle kick!

"GOOOOAAAALLLL!" screamed the mayor and Mr. Meow.

As soon as the Soccer Ball Monster hit the net, it burst open. Dynamo Dog and Lion L. Messy both fell to the ground. They had been tied up with rope. David Geckom also tumbled out and dropped a remote control.

"What's this?" Rider asked, picking the remote up.

He handed it to Westie, who pressed a button. The giant Soccer Ball Monster lurched forward then backward every time Westie used the remote. "Hey, this thing controls the Soccer Ball Monster!"

The group looked at David Geckom. The lizard smiled a mean smile. He shouted, "That's right. It was me!"

chapter
NINE

PENALTY
KICKS

"How could you?" Ziggy and Rora asked at the same time. The detectives, the mayor, Mr. Meow, and Frenchie surrounded the soccer star.

"The cost of fame is high," he said with a shrug. "I wanted to be the star of the championship game. But everyone loves Dynamo

Dog—so I had to get rid of him. I mean, how could soccer fans love a mascot more than the players?"

"Uh, becaussssse he'ssss totally awessssome," Mr. Meow said, to everyone's surprise.

"See?!" Geckom said. "So I dog-napped him to get him out of my

hair. While I wanted to win the championship for Pawston, I also wanted to be the MVP of the entire sport! So I got rid of Lion L. Messy to make certain the Catskills Cougars didn't stand a chance."

"How dare you, *ssssir!*" hissed Mr. Meow.

"I think we've heard enough," Rider said. He pulled a pair of handcuffs out, but before he could arrest Geckom, the swift gecko leaped over his head. Geckom ran toward the practice area where there were dozens of soccer balls.

One by one,
he started kicking them at
the detectives. Westie was
knocked back and so was
Rider. Ziggy and Rora dodged
the most shots, but even they
were no match for the soccer star
Geckom.

"He's got my vote for MVP!" Ziggy said, grabbing his sore head. "The Most Villainous Player!"

Frenchie escorted the mayor and Mr. Meow to safety, but when he went back to help the P.I. Pack, he was quickly knocked over by a soccer ball.

Geckom began laughing. "You

fools won't get anywhere near me. I can do this all day! I'm a soccer ball–kicking machine!"

"Kicking machine . . . ," Rider said. "That's it!" He grabbed Westie's remote control and used it to bring out the Kooky Kicker.

The machine marched onto the field and stood between the detectives and the villain. Then Rider switched it on, and the legs began kicking. "I may be no match for your soccer skills," Rider told Geckom, "but I think we have something that has a leg up on your kick tricks!"

Kick! Kick! Kick! Kick! Kick!

It was almost too amazing to believe as Geckom and the Kooky Kicker went into a soccer match frenzy! Hundreds of soccer balls were flying back and forth at incredible speeds. But even Geckom couldn't keep up with Westie's invention.

First one ball slipped past his
defense, then he was pummeled by
dozens more. Finally he threw up
his arms in surrender from under
a pile of soccer balls.

"Frenchie, would you like to do the honors?" Rider asked, handing over the set of handcuffs. Then the police dog held up a red card. "Mr. Geckom, you're ejected from the game and going to jail."

chapter TEN

GOOAAALLL!!!

At the beginning of the champion-ship game, there was a surprise award ceremony. The mayor gave the P.I. Pack and Frenchie special gold medals for helping to break the Goalie's Curse and saving the soccer match.

Pawston and Catskills fans cheered from the stands as the

detectives waved to the crowd. After the P.I. Pack stepped off the field, they were swarmed by reporters. Ziggy and Rora were the first to share their stories about how they solved the case.

However, Rider wasn't a fan of

all this attention. "This is the dog you want," Rider said as he pulled Frenchie in front of the cameras and microphones. "He's the real hero." The photographers surrounded the French bulldog and snapped hundreds of pictures.

As Rider walked off, Mr. Meow was waiting for him. The cat stuck out his paw, and the two shook. "If not for you and your team, thissss ssssoccer game would have been ruined. Thank you, Detective." Then the wealthy cat turned and retreated to his private box seats to watch the game.

Rider was shocked. Mr. Meow had never ever thanked him for solving a case.

Mr. Meow entered his luxury sky-kitty-box. As the richest cat

in town, he could afford the best
seats in the house, of course!
Inside the room, there was a fancy
spread of food, including catered
fish sticks, saucers of milk, and
caviar catnip.

He fixed himself a plate and then went to take his seat. There was only one other soccer fan in the giant room—Rotten Ruffhouse, the criminal rottweiler.

"Why are you smiling?" asked Rotten. "Rider ruined another one of your schemes."

"Hah!" Mr. Meow laughed. "I wasssss never part of thissss mad-capped mysssstery. True, I am a Cougarssss fan, and I want to win the championssssship. But I would never ssssstoop to ruining a soccer game. I may be a villain, but I have my honor."

"Really?" Rotten was shocked to hear that his diabolical boss didn't have his claws in this big-time soccer crime.

"Of coursssse," Mr. Meow said.

He put on a pair of dark sunglasses and smiled. "Now, let's enjoy this wonderful game today. Tomorrow, we'll go back to hatching more evil planssss."

CHECK OUT RIDER WOOFSON'S NEXT CASE!

"I have a package for Labra-cadabra-dor from Rider Woofson," said the delivery bird. He was a nervous bird. He'd never delivered a package to a prison before, let alone to The Cage—a prison that held only the most dangerous criminals.

"We'll take it from here," one

Excerpt from *Labra-cadabra-dor's Revenge*

of the prison guards said. He held the box up to his ear and gave it a little shake. "Well, it's not ticking. That's a good sign." Then the guard ran it through an X-ray machine. "Looks like we've got a cake."

"Run it through again," said the warden. "You can never be too sure when it comes to Labra. Before he was an inmate, that pesky pup was the world's most dangerous magical criminal."

The guard ran several more tests. He even opened the box. The cake had white frosting and a

Excerpt from *Labra-cadabra-dor's Revenge*

bunch of candy stars that spelled out "HAVE A MAGICAL DAY!"

"Cute," said the warden.

"The cake is safe, Boss," said the guard. "The only other thing in the box is a flimsy spoon."

The warden picked up the long spoon and examined it. "Okay, I'll deliver it myself."